Sea Wolf

First published 2016 by Bloomsbury Education,
an imprint of Bloomsbury Publishing Plc

50 Bedford Square, London, WC1B 3DP

www.bloomsbury.com

A CIP catalogue for this book is available from the British Library

ISBN 978 1 4729 2488 9

Printed in China by Leo Paper Products

1 3 5 7 9 10 8 6 4 2

Sea Wolf

KATHRYN WHITE

Inside illustrations by Frances Castle

BLOOMSBURY
LONDON OXFORD NEW YORK NEW DELHI SYDNEY

CONTENTS

Chapter One

It all happened after Dad left. That is when the trouble started.

My little brother Ethan began to act weird. He made up crazy stories. He lied at school about adventures he had been on with Dad.

Other kids would stop me and say, "Hey Maya, Ethan said he dived off Deer Canyon with your dad. Your little brother is such a liar!" or "Ethan told us that your dad had a fight with a black bear. Your little brother is a big loser."

Ethan's crazy stories did two things to me. They made me angry with him for telling lies and they made me angry with the kids who laughed at him.

I told Ethan to stop it. "Your crazy stories are making us look stupid," I said.

Ethan just grinned "No way. They love it!" he said.

When I spoke to Mum about it she said, "Ethan misses your dad. He will stop soon."

There it was again, the same old story. It was all about how Ethan missed Dad.

No one cared how I felt. I wished Ethan would get lost and never come back.

But it was one of Ethan's lies that sent us to Devil's Rock.

Chapter Two

I was going home from school when Ryan and his mates stopped me.

"Maya, listen to this. Ethan says he can kayak across the sea all the way to Devil's Rock," laughed Ryan.

His friends were all laughing. They sounded just like monkeys.

"Don't be stupid!" I snapped.

I pushed past them. I wanted to get away, but they came after me.

"How will he get past all those shipwrecks?" called Ryan. "In a sub?" His mates laughed. "And what about the monster that hides down there? Your little brother had better watch out for Sea Wolf. Rarrrr!"

"Get lost," I yelled. I tried to keep going but Ryan and his mates would **not** leave me alone.

"Hey, maybe he's got a speed boat. Then he would get to Devil's Rock and back in time to be tucked up with his teddy bear," said Ryan.

I turned round and faced him. He stopped dead.

"Leave him alone, will you?" I snapped, "He's just a little kid."

"He's a nerd," said Ryan.

My face burned red hot. I was really angry.

"Maybe he does tell lies. But the way you're picking on him stinks. Go and pick on someone your own size, bully," I hissed.

Ryan grinned. But I knew that I had made him feel small.

I stormed off.

Chapter Three

When I got home, Ethan was kicking his football about.

"You are so stupid!" I shouted. "Why did you tell Ryan that you could take a boat to Devil's Rock? You are making us look stupid."

Ethan's brown eyes went black. His hands turned to fists.

"Don't tell me what to do, little Miss Top-of-the-class," he yelled.

"Nobody goes to Devil's Rock. You are **crazy!**" I shouted. "Don't you know how many people have died there? The place is like a graveyard. It's full of wrecks. You are just a stupid liar!"

"All you ever do is get angry with me," Ethan shouted. "All you do is make me feel bad. You act like you hate me."

"I do hate you!" I shouted. I was so angry I wanted to punch Ethan right on the nose.

"I **can** go to Devil's Rock. Just get lost!" Ethan yelled. He kicked the ball away and ran off.

"Stop! Ethan!" I called.

Mum came into the garden. She was looking very tired.

"What's going on?" she asked.

"Nothing!" I said quickly. "We were just playing."

"Oh, I thought you two were fighting again," she said, frowning.

"No, we were only messing about," I said. I gave her a smile as sweet as honey.

"OK then," said Mum. She looked worried, but went back inside. As soon as the door closed behind her, I ran after Ethan.

I knew he was going to the boatyard. He always used to go there with Dad. What if he did try to get to Devil's Rock?

The sea around Devil's Rock was deadly. If Ethan took a boat out there he would drown for sure.

Chapter Four

In the autumn the weather can change any time. One minute the water is still, the next it is wild.

The sea around Devil's Rock is full of wrecked ships. It is a death trap.

Some people had even made a TV programme about it. They went down in a submarine. You could see broken, rusty ships.

I wasn't going to let Ethan go near those rocks.

So I chased him.

I was scared. I knew if we went hit those wrecks we would both sink into the deep, black water and never be seen again.

I wished I hadn't been so angry and shouted at Ethan.

Chapter Five

When I got to the boatyard, Ethan was already at sea. He was paddling a small, red kayak. My heart sank. There was no way he would get to Devil's Rock alive.

I waved and called to him, "Ethan, I'm sorry. Come back."

But he just put his head down and kept paddling.

I shouted again, but the noise of the sea crashing onto the rocks hid my cries.

I looked far out at the waves hitting Devil's Rock. I had to save my little brother.

I ran to the boat hut and grabbed the end of a big kayak. It was big enough for two people.

I dragged it down to the water. The cold sea washed over my feet and up my legs.

I pushed and pulled the big kayak out into the water until it floated. Then I tried to get in, but the kayak rolled over and tipped me out. The icy water made me gasp

I yelled and banged my fists on the water.

Then, I took hold of each side of the kayak. Slowly and carefully, I pulled myself in.

Once I was in the boat, I sat up and grabbed the paddle. I pulled it through the water, faster and faster I went, on and on until I could see Ethan up ahead.

I didn't know if it was because I was angry or if I was just frightened, but suddenly I began to cry.

Then, it hit me. I knew why I was crying. I was scared my little brother might drown.

Chapter Six

My kayak was bigger than Ethan's and I'm stronger than he is so I was faster.

As I got closer to Ethan, the water got darker and deeper. I looked up at the sky. It was grey. A storm was coming.

I shouted to Ethan, "Wait! Ethan, please wait."

He stopped paddling and floated on the rolling waves.

"Go back," he shouted.

"No. I'm not going back without you," I replied.

He watched me getting closer. Suddenly he put up his arm in fear and shouted, "Look out!"

I turned to look. as a giant wave hit me from the side. It sent me flying. The kayak flipped over and I was pulled down into the angry sea.

Chapter Seven

Each time I tried to swim up to the surface, the sea pulled me back down. I felt as if I was going to burst. I needed air. But there was only water.

Water ran up my nose and into my mouth. I was going to die. I was going to drown.

Then, something hit my shoulder. I reached up and grabbed at it. It was a paddle.

I felt Ethan pull me up as I kicked in the water. I came up gasping for air.

Ethan reached out and grabbed my arm. "It's OK, Maya. I've got you. Hang on!" he called.

Panting and gasping, I grabbed the side of the small kayak.

"You can't get in the kayak," he said, "It will tip over."

"Please, Ethan, I can't stay in the water. I'm so cold," I cried, "Please help me."

"Look!" said Ethan. He pointed at the big kayak. It was floating upside down on the water. "We have to get to it and turn it right way up. You swim and I'll paddle."

I looked across the waves and saw the big kayak bobbing upside down.

"I can go and get it," I said.

"No," shouted Ethan, "You might get swept away. Stay with me, Maya. Hang on. We can go together."

He reached out and touched my ice-cold hand. "We can do it," he said.

Something in Ethan had changed. He seemed more grown up. Suddenly I felt safe with him.

He started to paddle towards the big kayak. I swam and pushed the little kayak in front of me. Ethan leaned away from me to keep the kayak moving in a straight line. We wobbled and paddled hard. We were getting closer and closer.

Hold on," said Ethan, "I can grab it."

I heard a crunch as the kayaks bumped together. Ethan put his legs over the side and slid into the sea.

His small kayak rolled into me. I cried out.

"Hang on, Maya," he called. Then he disappeared under the water.

"Come back," I screamed.

My heart raced. I could feel it thumping in my chest. I clung to the kayak, but my body was turning to ice.

Ethan had gone.

Chapter Eight

Suddenly, the big kayak flipped over. Ethan was sitting in one of the seats, holding the paddle.

"Here," he cried. "Let go and take my hand."

I pushed the small kayak away and reached out.

Ethan grabbed my icy fingers and pulled me towards the big kayak. He put my hand around the side. I held on but I was so tired and cold I could hardly move.

"I can't get in," I cried.

"Pull yourself across the kayak so you are lying over the middle" said Ethan. "Then swing your legs round."

I reached over with one hand and pushed myself up with the other.

Ethan grabbed my tee shirt and dragged me in. The kayak rocked madly. “Wait,” cried Ethan, “Or the kayak will roll.”

A wave swept under us.

I lay face down, looking into the deep, black water around us. I did not have the strength to pull myself in. Then Ethan called, “Do it now, Maya, swing your legs in.”

It took all of my energy to pull my legs into the boat. I lay back and rested on Ethan.

"You did it!" Ethan shouted. I felt a small smile form on my frozen lips.

"How did you turn the big kayak the right way up?" I asked.

"Dad showed me how to do it," Ethan said, proudly.

Suddenly, there was a crack of thunder. Lightning flashed and the kayak bounced up over the waves and back down. Ethan paddled to try to keep us steady. I closed my eyes as the rain beat at us.

Ethan paddled faster, trying to push us back towards land.

"The sea is pulling us towards Devil's Rock, Maya," he said.

I looked to my left and saw a blue fork of lightning shoot across the sky. Devil's Rock flashed into a strange shape.

"We have to get away," I called. "The sea near the rock is too dangerous."

"I know," cried Ethan, "Sea Wolf will find us. I know it is there, I just know it."

He paddled as hard as he could. The rain beat down. I could not see land. Ethan pushed on. I knew that he would not be able to keep this up for long. He was getting tired.

"No! Come on, we are winning!" I shouted. I felt a bit stronger. I just had to help.

But I was too late. A gust of wind pushed us back. Then a huge black wave hit us hard.

We flew into the air. I closed my eyes.

"No!" Ethan yelled.

We crashed down into the black sea. I tried to cry out but salty water rushed into my mouth.

Devil's Rock had beaten us.

We went under.

Chapter 9

I was too weak and cold to swim. I tried to keep my head above water but I could feel myself sinking lower and lower. I tried to look for Ethan but I couldn't see him. He had gone.

Then, I saw a horrible sight.

A strange beast was speeding through the water. It was coming right at me. The beast had bright green eyes. It opened its mouth and I saw its white teeth. I thought about the horror stories of Sea Wolf.

Was this Sea Wolf?

It opened its mouth wider. Its head grew bigger and stranger as it came closer. I tried to scream but my mouth filled with cold sea water.

I closed my eyes and felt the monster sink its teeth into my sleeve. Then, my body was pulled, higher and higher until my head was out of the water. The monster dragged me, on and on through the wild water. Suddenly felt myself being pulled out.

When I opened my eyes I was lying on the deck of a small boat. A huge black beast was standing above me.

A man said, "Well done, Blue. Clever girl!" He turned to me. "Are you OK?" he said, "does it hurt anywhere?"

"I'm fine," I said and looked up. Ethan was sitting, wrapped up in a blanket. The beast walked over to him and sat down.

"Maya," Ethan cried. "Is she going to be alright?" he asked the man.

"She'll be fine," said the man, "She's safe now."

I breathed in the cold sea air. I was alive. Ethan was alive. I felt a wave of happiness wash over me.

Tears rolled down Ethan's cheeks. "Maya, we made it," he said.

I sat up and saw that the beast was a huge, shaggy black dog.

It was wet and pools of water were dripping onto the deck of the boat. It had bright green eyes. It looked like a wonderful, wet, cuddly bear.

"Hello Maya. I'm Adam, from the coastguard. And this is our brave Blue," said the man. He pointed at the dog. "You are lucky kids. Blue saved you both. Now we must get you back to dry land. Your mum will be worried sick. The doctor is waiting to check you are OK. Then we need to get you home."

Blue bent down and licked my cheek and I reached up and hugged her and then Ethan.

I cried all the way home but not because I was sad. That day was the happiest day of my life. After that, things changed for me and Ethan. We were not just brother and sister; we were best friends too.

Ethan's happier now. Adam lets him help at the rescue hub. I don't think he misses Dad quite as much as he did. And me? I help to take good care of Blue.

She is the most amazing rescue dog in the whole world and Ethan is the most amazing brother.

Bonus Bits!

Interesting Words

You might not know some of the words in the story as they relate to boats and the sea. Have a look below if you need help.

boatyard – area of land where boats are built and stored, enclosed with a fence to keep the boats safe

coastguard – people who keep watch on the sea around the coast. They help people and ships that are in danger, and look out for criminals moving things in or out of the country

kayak – canoe with a light frame and a covering to keep the water out. It has a small opening in the top that you can sit in

paddle – a short pole that has a flat blade at one or both ends. It is used to move a small boat or canoe through the water

submarine – a ship that has a special hull that allows it to go under water for long periods of time

Kathryn White

Here are some fascinating and surprising facts about the author of this book.

Kathryn White lives in Wells which is the smallest city in Britain

She wrote her first children's story when her own child was 1 year old

Her first story was never published but it gave her the interest and enthusiasm to write more

Kathryn says she writes little notes on pieces of paper about her story ideas as she goes about her daily life

She has written over 20 stories and poems now. She has even written some ghost stories!

Her stories usually have animals in as either the main character or a key character

Rescue Dogs

In this story the coastguard use a rescue dog to help save the children. But do they really use dogs?

YES – the coastguard in places like Canada and Italy use dogs to help them

Here are some interesting facts about the dogs:

- they are Newfoundland dogs
- they are very calm

- they LOVE water
- they see it as a game rather than work

Even though the dogs enjoy their work, they have to train for 3 years before they can help the coastguard.

Once trained they:

- jump from helicopters
- jump from boats
- rush into the sea from the shore

Painting Pictures

The author has used lots of creative language to paint pictures in the readers' heads. Here are a few examples:

'rolling waves'

'angry sea'

'my body was turning to ice'

'crack of thunder'

'lightning flashed'

'the kayak bounced up over the waves'

'the sea is pulling us'

'the rain beat down'

'wild water'

'a wave of happiness washed over me'

When doing your own writing try to paint pictures in your reader's heads with the language you use.

Next Steps

Why not write your own story about an animal that saves a human? Here are some people who might need saving to give you a starting point!

A rock climber who has fallen.

A person on a sinking boat.

Someone who is stuck on some rocks when the tide has come in.